No Savannah Sunrise

Artie Sparks

Noir Adventure.

Prologue

Cole James worked for the law firm of Alvin, Norman, and Swan for a while. The law firm partners were in active debate in their conference room. They were discussing the effectiveness of decisions that they made in a current case. A young lawyer's performance in his first court action was also being evaluated by them.

They all made comments to that effect. None of them thought badly of his work. Josh Swan was impressed with Cole. "It seems that James is showing that he is up to the job."

Gary Alvin agreed with that. He replied. "Yes, I agree, I like the way that he turns a question around on his opposition."

The meeting carried on for a while longer. Much was said about him, and the cases that he handled. Lydia Norman got to the point of the issue to put an end to the discussion. "I think that we're all saying that we are in agreement to stick with James."

"I think that one of us should spend part of the day in court with him in case he needs some backup advice," Alvin said.

"I agree," Norman said.

"Let's take turns in court," Swan said, and they were satisfied with the results of the meeting.

* * *

Cole noticed that the firm partners were still meeting when he left the office for the day. He stopped off for food at a Henry near the law office.

He ate one of their fish dishes cooked in wine sauce stuffed with leeks

and prawns in brandy and cream sauce
with lots of garlic.

Then he went to a sports bar and
pool hall near there. He dropped by for
a nightcap and to celebrate his bar
certification some more.

However, he was joined
unexpectedly by Doug. He had been
drinking there for a while, when Cole
arrived. "Well Cole ole pal, you don't
get out much since you became an
ambulance chaser."

"Doug boy, God love yah."

"I thought that you would do your
share of drinking while you practiced
the law. But, you're never here with
any of us."

"I'll drink to that," Molly the bartender said.

"Molly, I will have a double-bourbon, and get Doug a drink as well," Cole said and he kissed her.

"Here's to the law won't keep you out of here again," Doug said as a toast.

"You can say that, or I am a junior ambulance chaser."

"What does that mean?"

"It simply means that I work long hours," they chatted and drank for a while.

As they were chatting two women came through the bar front door also laughing and chatting. The women were

Joan, a friend of Doug's, and another woman. Joan introduced the other woman, Minnie, to Cole. Doug already knew Minnie. "Hi, Doug!"

"Cole, this is Minnie," Joan did the introducing.

Cole sat with Minnie for a while at the bar where they drank and talked. Her voice was soft and delicate. She was not the wild woman type that was normally associated with Cole and Doug. Cole and Minnie chatted for a while, laughed about a few things, and they were getting along just fine.

Chapter 1

        Six months earlier, Cole James had
been a law clerk with the law firm
Alvin, Norman, and Swan for a while.
However, his firm only knew him as bar

certified for that one day. Then he
went missing ever since then.

Police believed that what he
witnessed resulted in his abduction and
murder. They believed that he saw the
robbery of a store on Woodlawn Street
that occurred overnight, and he was
killed because he could identify the
robber.

The police believed that robberies
at a motel, and a convenience store
were committed by that murderer.
However, that case had been bogged down
without a clue. Then it went completely
cold.

Savannah Police detectives just
finished gathering evidence from their
investigation of those few store

robberies that just occurred overnight. The investigations' state police lieutenant went over the evidence as they organized it for review. It was the second set of such crimes across the street from one another in six months.

The lieutenant looked over what was collected. He thought that the break-ins came from the heavily wooded alley like the robbery and abduction of six months ago.

The criminals tried to avoid dropping anything that might have their DNA. But several items were gathered that might have some usable trace evidence.

He notified his captain about that before sunrise. The captain thought about it. Then he replied. "This is a second chance to catch the same criminal from across the street, the motel, and convenience store as well."

"You think both sets of crimes could be the same suspect?"

"Yes, this is not a neighborhood that has been typically full of hoods. That is why I think it could be one person that committed all these crimes. The predator came in through the alley behind Woodlawn Street in all the cases."

"Get real answers from the investigators. That will provide our solution."

"Okay, we need one of our state police investigator here. Send a detective behind these building. Have them find something with trace evidence on it."

* * *

It was the inner city of Savannah, not far from the Atlantic Ocean and the railroad before that to the east, and the Savannah River to the south. Wally Flore grew up in the neighborhood where he worked as a police detective.

Children that came from there used to buy homes there when they became adults. They did so to live closer to their parents. The tall-strapping man was one of those children, now with thinning blonde hair.

The main shopping places that were up Woodlawn Street were mostly small shops. There were several women's and men's clothing shops, a Henry, a bakery, a cleaners, a food market, and a meat market conducting business along there.

Most industrial jobs were long gone from there. However, it had some small businesses, a plumber, an air condition repair shop, and some industry that seemed to remain in business there. There was also a slaughterhouse beyond that. That was much of the local employment.

There was also some landscaping,
and some public playgrounds and sports
fields. Beyond the shops and small
industrial areas were more housing, a
bar and small eateries.

The sports playing field was up
Woodlawn Street beyond the Flore's
house. Most of that was near the
railroad yards, and then there was Cole
James's apartment building along Shore
Drive, and Atlantic Ocean. The Savannah
Police patrolled it all from one
station.

However, Ida and her parents were
different from those that came from
there. They once moved from here to
Atlanta.

Her older sister was losing her home in Savannah after refinancing it. The variable interest loan got out of hand by doing that.

Their parents managed to buy out the foreclosure problem and sold the Atlanta house as well. They are all living in Savannah now. They also live in the same neighborhood as the detective.

They all lived together in the neighborhood about a year. Then Ida followed them here recently. They in that large house near the sea.

* * *

Wally Flore saw Ida while she was window shopping on Woodlawn Street. She saw nothing that caught her eye and she stopped at looking.

Then she started walking her way to the bakery. She hoped to purchase some bake goods prior to returning home to her parents' house.

He was coming out of that wooded area behind the stores. She noticed that he was strangely coming from there. She was unaware that it was an old crime scene.

He was not sure that criminals entered and exited the scene through that wood area when he first saw her. He had been searching for evidence that could tie the cases together with

criminals coming and going by using
those woods.

She noticed he came out that wood
area behind those buildings. She
wondered why anyone, other a workman,
would be back there. She gave him a
strange look not aware what he was
doing there.

Here, he was a well-dressed man
that was in an alley. Then she saw that
there was yellow tape on some store
doors, and police barricading, and any
unmarked police car there.

Then she realized that the
Savannah Police were across the street
investigating something. Later, she
learned about the robberies, at the two
stores next to the bakery, that

occurred overnight. She thought that he must have something to do with that.

The police finished gathering evidence a while ago. Their cars began to leave the crime scene. However, the investigators of the robberies were still discussing some matters about catching the criminals.

Detective Flore was not working with them. He came on the scene independently looking over the cold cases. He hoped to discover an object with some trace evidence that indicated that that crime was related to the stores on either side of the bakery that were just robbed overnight.

He had been going over the evidence documentation from the old

crime scene of six months ago, and in
the alley for anything that might have
been missed back then.

They found a putty knife with
blood on it at last night's crime scene
behind those buildings. The intruder
cut himself using the tool to break in
the second store.

The criminal dropped the tool
running out that wooded alley. The
criminal then failed to retrieve it in
that thickly wooded place.

Flore found an iPod at the old
murder scene. It had been lodged in
dirt covered with weeds by a wheel of a
dumpster.

It appeared that the killer
dropped it in the struggle with the
victim. It fell in the crack, and the
killer or victim stepped on it pushing
it deeper in the crack.

* * *

Wally Flore finished his
assignment for the day. However, he
continued puttering around like he was
being neighborly even though he was
still on duty. That behavior was
something that his commander did not
like about him.

He gave the impression that he was
hard nose at times, but it was mostly a
bluff. The real guy was outgoing,

friendly, and passed many off-duty hours browsing the neighborhood chatting with people in stores, and on the street.

He was sailing Atlantic Ocean on a rented boat shared with friends. Or he was at the sports bar and pool hall up the street.

He often told stories with quite inventive humorous lies. He also sang old rock-a-Billie songs while shooting darts or playing pool. He had always been a friendly guy.

He entered Webb's Bakery with a plan to have a warm roll for breakfast and have some to take home. He got in line standing behind the people that were in line or already ordering their baked goods. Other customers were still chatting with one another after they made their purchases.

He moved to the front of the line before long, after a long wait. He still had ordering some rolls on his mind. Then he saw Ida again, when she entered the bakery, and he offered her his place in the line. "Here, you order first. I can wait."

"Oh, you were in the alley a while ago. What were you doing there?"

"I'm a policeman on duty. I am investigating some robberies."

"Oh yes, there were robberies across the street. Did you catch the bad guy?"

"No, not yet."

"Oh, but one thing, you were in the alley on this side of the street. I don't understand how you could be doing that on the wrong side of the street."

"Yes, I was still investigating the robberies that happened last night?"

"Well, whatever."

"What are you ordering?"

"French bread and some rolls."

"Did you know about the lovely rolls that they bake here?"

"Yes, my parents love them. Someone must really love you for buying them too."

"Yes, my mother, but she really loves me most when I breakout with a song."

"Oh really? You're not going to do it here?"

"Yes, this is a fine place for a song," and he began singing a tune.

"That was lovely," she would never do that, and other customers were waiting.

"We must not allow these folks to wait," and they let other customers move ahead of them in line too.

They were not in the least bit alike except they both liked warm rolls from that bakery. She was an average height, brunette, serious and shy. His fair hair was thinning, but he was still tall and strapping.

Wally had an idea as they moved to the back of the line. He recalled the food at the Henry nearby there. "The food in the place near here has a fine breakfast, and great chicken. They cook their fish dishes in wine sauce stuffed with leeks and prawns in brandy and cream sauce with lots of garlic."

"You seem to know the place well."

"I know the neighborhood."

"Are you inviting me for a meal?"

"That's right, yes I am."

"I'll have a warm roll with coffee now, and I could use a salad later."

"They have that. So, it is late morning. Their salad is a regular garden salad, but it also consists of little radishes, and feathering tops of spring onions. Let's skip the rolls for another time and have brunch there."

"Okay, all this food talk has made me hungry."

"I grew up in this neighborhood. However, now I'm a policeman here."

"The only thing you're working on is me."

"Not at all, I have my eyes open."

* * *

It is in the beginning, they seemed to get along famously. They saw most things the same way. She seemed to have a heart of gold. She did not know him well enough to have much devotion toward him. They were getting along just the same.

* * *

Detective Flore and Ida entered the Henry together for an early lunch, not brunch. They saw the breakfast cook as they entered and greeted him. "Bobby good morning."

"This is Ida; she's new to the neighborhood."

"Hello, nice to have both of you here."

"It's nice to meet you," Ida said.

"What brought you out, Wally?"

"That lawyer, Cole James that disappeared six-months ago is a cold case now. I'm looking for new evidence because of these two robberies last night."

"Oh, the robberies."

"Does it worry you that this robber is still out there?"

"I suppose it does. I arrive while it's still dark."

"No sunrise for you?"

"That's right, none for me. It's worrisome that there are no suspect to any it."

"Maybe we'll catch him soon."

"Really?"

"Yeah, you know Cole was here the night that he disappeared. You saw him here, right."

"Yes, we booth had a late dinner here. I talked to him just as I was leave for home."

"I remember him being here," Sharon the waitress said butting into their chat.

***THEN SHE TOLD HER STORY

ABOUT THE NIGHT COLE

JAMES DISAPPEARED***

"Cole told me about the boat he
sailed on Atlantic Ocean a week
earlier. He said that the entire crew
survived the boat wreck with minor
injuries and were hospitalized only
overnight. But they were all unemployed
waiting for the skipper to get a new
boat. He told me that he loved the
ocean side part of town, particularly
its sunrises. He often sat out on his
apartment balcony watching it in the
morning. As a student, he came in here
while going to law school. He did all
of his higher education not far from
here."

"What was the big deal of him coming here that night?" Flore asked.

"He celebrated for months after he finished taking the law bar examination. Then he learned that he passed it, and just became a bar certified lawyer. He came here for our chicken before he went out to celebrate his bar certification at the bar across the street." Flore knew the drill about the case from there. James went home after several hours at the bar, never heard of again.

***THEN SHE STOPPED TELLING

HER JAMES STORY***

Chapter 2

The detective had breakfast and coffee with his parents the next morning. They sipped more coffee after that, and his parents each smoked a cigarette after they finished while drinking more coffee.

They spoke about the Cole James may be reopened. Then his parents were done smoking at the kitchen table. His father said. "Wally should leave that case alone."

"They work the case hard enough." his mother replied. "No evidence, no witnesses and no suspects. Wally, suppose they you the case."

"Yes," their togetherness was over-with and he left there.

* * *

Wally Flore saw Ida home after a long morning and lunch together. Then he went to his office. He was, twenty-five years old, still lived with his parents in that small three-bedroom house with close proximally to their next-door neighbors.

Then Wally entered the kitchen after he arrived home. He greeted his parents. He spoke to his father first. "Dad, you're quiet this morning."

"He was up late last night," his mother replied.

Wally however put them both in the mood that they had no concern for what anyone thought about such personal problems. His father replied. "Well, the hell with it! I'm going to have a great day."

"Sure," they both said.

"I'll have an early lunch at the Henry," Wally replied, and Betty left for another room to take care of something.

"Your father is going to say that the owners, the Robby's, are getting divorced."

"His drinking and gambling I suppose," his father answered the question.

"Already?"

"It was a whirlwind marriage," his father replied.

"Yeah, I suppose so. What do you know about those bookies that hangout there?"

"It seems that there is one. Some stupid kid that has parents that own that motel that got robbed six months ago."

"Jim Collen."

"That's him."

"Do you know who he works for?"

"He hangs around with the owners sometimes. This guy is too young for retirement, and he has no sign of having a real job."

"He could be connected."

"I heard that he's from Cleveland, and some kind of criminal."

"Is he running around with the Don Robby's wife?"

"No, she's been running around with someone else."

"That is interesting." Wally replied. "I must get a few hours' sleep, Dad. Then the lieutenant has scheduled a meeting with me in the late afternoon."

"Sure kid."

* * *

Wally woke as he planned in the late afternoon. He entered the kitchen a short while later, greeting them. He spoke to his father first. "Dad, you're quiet for being here," and he did not answer him, and his mother seemed moody too.

Wally walked out of the house, and his father took that as a queue. Thus, he followed him out the door moments later. Her mood changed again with that. She yelled at her husband before

the door slammed behind him. "You damn
bastard!"

"A damn bastard having a great
day." He remarked, and she knew that
she lost her grip on him. "The late
owners of that diner were our friends.
She is annoyed that the police can't
nail any bad guys."

"You mean me?"

"You too."

Wally's father lit up a cigarette
outside the house; then he went
straight to the coffee shop from there.
He thought of the place and corner bar
as his real home.

His drinking buddies were friends
to him even though he never saw them

outside there on occasion; however, she was kind of cheating too.

* * *

Later that day, the DNA found on the iPod and putty knife matched when compared. However, it matched no one that was known to the police as being the usual suspects or anyone on the FBI's data base.

The captain did not have the real answers from the investigators that would provide an immediate solution. The captain was up against the wall with the mayor, police commissioner, and city council.

Many neighbors were worried now. They felt safe and protected living there for years, but that was no more. There was fear that the criminal would abduct someone else and take more lives.

The lieutenant was desperate to get the cases moving toward the solutions, when he met with his captain. The captain had a stern look when they came face to face. He clearly felt the heat from the powers above too. "Lieutenant, those cases, on and near Woodlawn Street, was not solved as of yesterday. Now we have more. There were items found with matching DNA at each scene. We have no suspect to compare it with."

"It has been hard for my people to follow up on leads on suspects with the FBI not keeping us in the loop."

"These crimes are still capital with the murder, and not federal. How come you're counting on the FBI?"

"We don't know if there is a murder. The abduction is federal. We hoped that the FBI had a few potential suspects, and they tell us nothing about what they know."

"I don't believe this excuse. We have local robberies here. You're telling me that we can't solve these after a long morning. cases because the FBI won't do your job for you? The commissioner is supposed to tell the mayor and city council that?"

"So far, we cannot tie anyone to a murder or knowing anything about where they might be even though we have several DNA from Henry. We don't his DNA to match it with at a crime scene. Captain, we still have nothing without a body."

"That's all you have?"

"Yes, sir, that is it."

He got an answer that he did not want to hear about the abduction, and he also needed know what was stalling the investigation of a number of motel and convenience store robberies along the beach highway strip, and not a suspect for nearly a year. "You can't blame the FBI for any of the motel and convenience store thefts."

"You know that transients move in out of Savannah like a revolving door."

"City council doesn't want to hear talk about unknown transients as suspects. This Cole James was abducted by someone he knew, not a transient."

"We try to run them out of town before they can commit crimes, but there are too many of them that move in and then skip town."

"You need to solve some of these cases fast and having nothing won't wash."

"We're trying."

They both knew that they needed to expand the investigation in order to get the results that they needed. The captain explained it regarding his budget. "I told you before about overtime and other manpower. You need to do more with what we have. After all, we do have some budget for this, not much, but some."

"I know, and I'm adding another detective to work these cases."

"What will another detective add to these cases?"

"It's Wally Flore. He brings experience with the neighborhood, he's from there."

The captain knew the drill with crimes when so many people are coming and going here with the economy so poor. Other neighborhoods were rougher,

and historically had more crime, and
more of the cases had gone cold. He
wanted to keep crime status quo at the
worst.

He was clearly unhappy with what
happened in this neighborhood with the
five robberies, and the abduction. The
captain shook his head like to say no,
and then nodded yes. "I guess this is
the only choice, and I have to make
this extra detective sound good to the
powers to be."

"Yes sir," The lieutenant was at a
loss not to agree and knew that he
could only hope to get good detective
work from his people with so much lost
time.

"Make sure he remembers that he is investigating, and not partying with his friends instead of working the case."

"Yes sir." Then they say goodbye.

The lieutenant sat back at his office and pondered over how to get the badly needed answers to solve these cases. He told the captain a good story. Still, he never thought that Detective Flore would be of any real help in the case. He did choose him to help despite all his concerns because his desperation was so overwhelming.

He was also quite concerned, and reluctant to use him in time consuming assignments, even with the benefits of his vast experience in that neighborhood. He knew Flore as being a dedicated officer, and he could also forget that he was even working a case being sociable.

He hoped that Wally Flore will remember that he was born in that Savannah, Georgia neighborhood. He knew his parents as working-class people that were also there all their lives. He had arrested his father, a retired merchant sailor, as an officer, when he was drunk, and disorderly. He coached all three sons raised by Joe and Betty Flore as boys in sports.

* * *

Neighborhood dwellers that visited where Cole James would go did not mind the rough chat. Nor did they have concerns about drug use in the bathrooms.

Woodlawn Street was the main street of the neighborhood. There stood a Church on one corner, the bank on another, a pharmacy on another, and a bar was on the fourth corner.

* * *

Detective Flore's father was often quite drunk when he arrived home at night. Years ago, he usually came home from the bar before his sons came home from school as boys. Back then, once

they arrived home, he treated them with
his arrogant tongue.

He still did that to them, all
grown men, when he saw any of them.
They did not care about his arrogance
or what he felt about anything.

Wally once had the same hard
feelings toward their father as his
brothers. However, he thought of him as
his best friend now, a pathetic drunk
or not.

Joe was at the bar all day. He did
not give attention to what else was
going on there. Then he saw a stranger
enter the bar. He walked to a bar stool
and sat down. The bartender, nearly as
drunk as Joe, asked for his order.
"What will you have, sir?"

"I'll have a vodka tonic."

He poured his drink for him. He said. "Here you are, sir."

"Thanks."

"Is there anything else, sir?"

"No, you lush," he drank quietly for a few minutes until he saw a lovely lady. Then he took the stool next to her.

Joe did not notice a man pressing that woman in the bar for sex that she did not want. He still did not show concern for her being angry over the guy's attention. Then she yelled. "Get away from me!"

"I'm the only man you should want!"

"What? You're sure in love with yourself! Get away from me! Go away now!" the guy left her alone.

Her voice was not heard over the loud music. So, the guy felt no need to stop. Her temper went off the charts as she heard more of his arrogance. She remarked. "You're the jerk who that hit on Sally that time!"

"Whom the hell is Sally?"

"Well, keep your distance from me, you bastard!"

Some girls would rather have just died than utter such words as she did so boldly toward the appalling young man. Here, she now discovered that it

was not at all in private, but in front
of the bar drunks.

"Oh sure, I remember a wretched
bitch like you," she smacked his face,
he did her back and the tender was busy
paid much to misbehaving.

"You damn bastard!" she held her
sore face.

The bar tender noticed that she
held face. The guy that hit her replied
to that. "Don't concern yourself.
She'll soon sweetened up."

"Are you sure?"

"She rough toward me before and I
did her."

She had enough of that and left
there. She walked out of the bar with

him behind her. He followed her to the outside. She screamed at him thinking he was stalking her. "Please go away from me!"

He grabbed her by the throat. He yelled. "You are a stupid bitch."

"You bastard!

She threw her hand up to smack him again, he caught her hand, and she screamed some more. He held her hearing enough of the screaming.

She failed to stop screaming. So, he punched her in her face. His hard punch landed square on her jaw. He beat her some more before anyone knew what was happening.

He looked around him, and saw
that no one was near him, thinking that
there were no witnesses. He kicked her
in the midsection and rushed away
walking fast at first. He was gone from
the scene.

The guy had run away from where he
parked his car as well. He felt that if
he tried to escape by car, he would
have to run two blocks to get too it.

He felt that he might only need to
hide out somewhere in some barn
overnight. Then he would retrace his
steps back to his car in the morning
while it is still dark.

Besides only the victim knew his
identification. He thought that the
bartender seemed too drunk to make an

accurate identification. Still, he thought the victim might identify him eventually.

Then he ran for several blocks away from there. He left her bleeding doing that. He thought the police would check the alleys, so he avoided them. He went up street undiscovered. He was doing good making his escape.

* * *

Some key evidence against him in a previous arrest warrant was mailed in error while it was being checked into the police evidence room some time ago. It got mixed up with the outgoing mail that was mistakenly sent to the wrong address. The police still hoped for its

recovery. Then the post office

delivered it to the wrong address out

of state. That mail was returned to the

post office as misdirected.

Then the mistakes were not over

yet. It sat in a hamper at the post

office for an afternoon. Next, it was

checked over, and determined that it

had the police department address. So,

it was loaded in a mail truck ready to

go back to them.

However, the truck was already too

full. So, they unloaded the last items

that were put on the truck and that

evidence was among that payload. It sat

in another hamper to await loading on a

truck.

The last hamper that was removed from that truck was placed next to items that were being sent toward Florida. Then everything there was loaded on the same truck.

The evidence went well south with that regular mail. It became misdirected mail once again when it showed up in a large State of Florida Government mail room.

There, the evidence was found by a worker, and it was discovered that it was covered with postal stickers on the address and return address. Thus, all of that was returned to the post office once again.

When that mail arrived there, it was inspected. There was no way that

the evidence could now be considered
anything other than lost in the mail.
Thus, that evidence was against lost in
the mail forever.

Still, they hope that enough of
the lost mail will be recovered so that
some of the prior warrant charges on
him will stick.

The Savannah Police could not know
that about the permanently lost mail.
They hoped that the lost outstanding
warrant on the suspect would resurface.
Then again with that being so, the
police still had other outstanding
warrants on him, and there will be more
charges against him soon.

* * *

Then someone saw a small puddle of blood outside the bar on Woodlawn Street. The blood trail led them to a woman trying to get on her feet. She seemed able to do so. "Ma'am, what happened?"

"The bastard…" She tried to talk, and she fell out cold on the ground.

The escaping guy kept running. He now felt that he needed to get out of that neighborhood fast. The suspect that otherwise police will be chasing him down soon.

* * *

Doug also saw the woman on the ground from a window, and he called for help. He realized that the woman had obviously been beaten rather badly. Then he called Wally Flore for help. Soon the Savannah Police and Paramedics arrived on the scene of the woman that had been beaten not long after they received that call. The police found the victim out cold on the sidewalk.

There were no eyewitnesses, except some confused drunks including the bartender. No one near the crime scene had seen anyone running away from there at all. The officers tried to catch the assailant with patrol cars up the streets believing that he would be on

foot running away toward his truck or
car from there.

Officers in patrol cars began to
search up and down streets near
Woodlawn Street for the man who had
fled the crime scene. They were having
no luck with that. No one saw anyone
running away from there at all. So that
pursuit of finding an assailant had
failed quickly.

His lucky would be better if he
saw a barn or garage on a farm. The
police were going everywhere except the
right places to pursue him trying to
catch him for this crime. He ran out of
towns roads. He felt that he can head
directly the first farm he sees.

Then the police brought the county sheriff in on the search checking farms such similar places. But then the guy saw a patrol car with flashing lights rounding a corner toward a farm.

The guy ran in the woods. The guy was sure now that his only means of escape from the area must start by sleeping in a nearby barn.

He kept walking through woods until he saw a from farmhouse with barn behind it. He emerged from the woods and walked toward the barn.

When he reached there, he then expected to stay only until morning. He thought he better wake and leave there while it is still dark.

He entered the barn with that plan mind. He saw that there was no concrete floor. He slept on such a hard surface. His was still sore for days. He was glad for that when he saw the dirt floor.

He bedded down immediately. He thought about where to go from there for only a few moments. Then Wally Flore commented. "Don't get too restful."

The guy jumped to his holding his fisted hand to take punch at him. He did that for just an instant. He only did until he saw the gun in Flore's hand. Then he said. "Damn!"

"I'm glad you stood up."

"What?"

"It's easier to put handcuffs on this way."

* * *

His lieutenant was happy that Flore arrested a suspect for anything. He now saw Flore as a serious detective. He hoped to have the same success with the motel and convenience store robberies cases when he assigned him to do undercover work.

He was no longer desperate about those cases despite that the investigations have produced nothing. He believed that with proper surveillance from Flore that he could

stop the robbers from striking again.

Chapter 3

The lieutenant felt that Wally's whole life made him best suited to solve these cases after he made that arrest. He thought that the predator may even be someone that the detective knew well.

He called Detective Flore to his office to inform him of his decision. The detective made some remarks as he entered the office. He said. "Sir, are we going out on the lake fishing or something?"

The lieutenant did not see any time off until after they break the backs of the cases. "That sounds good, detective. These cases may use up too much of our time for anything else for a while."

"I thought that might be the case
after I took that fellow out of that
barn," they chatted some more, and had
a few laughs.

The lieutenant quickly got down to
business about the problem at hand. He
asked the detective to handle a part of
the case. "Well, detective we need that
kind of effort again."

"Sir, what can I do?"

"I need your help in a way that
you might think of as unconventional."

"What assignment do you want me to
handle?"

"I need your full time help with
of these robbers. Your task will be

sort of undercover, and you just being
you."

"Yes sir."

"Fine, I think that we understand
one another."

He felt particularly confident
with Flore being a fresh look at the
investigation. After he has not worked
the case from the beginning when the
crimes occurred.

Besides, he lived nearby there. He
was a detective with the confidence of
his recent success. Him sending this
detective out on these case now was at
least saving face. The detective asked
about that. "What specifically are you
planning?"

"Detective, my plan involves case
that gone old. I want you to work on
the motel and convenience stores
robberies. You'll go undercover to find
out what happened to that lawyer after
that."

"Cole James."

"Correct."

Flore was also aware that these
cases have been going nowhere. He
remarked. "None of cases have any
evidence or suspects."

"That's correct too."

He felt that the lieutenant had
been feeling the heat from his
superiors for a while. He said. "Sir,

you want that lawyer's killer bad,
right?"

"There is no body yet. So, it's
him and his abductor. Did I hit a nerve
with you too?"

"Yes sir. It's not you."

"Listen Detective, spend your time
relaxing at these beach side spots
undercover."

"The stores, and the motel there?"

"Yes, enjoy being yourself
poolside and mingling this weekend.
Some of the people by the motel pool
are from your neighborhood. See if any
of them can provide some leads to
suspects."

"Most of them know me. They always talk of some police matters when they see me."

"Well, that could be helpful. So, there are some other benefits for putting you on this case. Do it until you get a lead, and then eat up this case."

"I think you're on to something, sir. I'll catch some rays out at the motel pool deck this afternoon."

"Then that's it, enjoy it."

"I hope I don't have to jail my friends doing this."

"Criminals are criminals."

This was clearly Flore's most affective kind of assignment, where he can mix in with people that are having

a good time. He said. "I feel that

these folks in the neighborhood love to

hear detective business."

"Don't speak that way."

"They are my people."

"Okay, I suppose they are. Now

Detective; let's get these cases off

the books."

* * *

Flore left his commander's headed

for being beside the sea. He went there

with what was said at the meeting still

on his mind.

Then he arrived in that beach sea
place. He thought about pretending
being something he is not. Then he was
in front of some of his neighbors who
were at that motel pool.

Then he someone that he arrested
at least one time an officer. Why would
anyone in this place will think of me
as a tourist? To them, I'll clear being
doing surveillance as I catch some rays
on the pool deck.

He thought, if I try to piece
together some lying story, someone will
tell the others the truth. My tell the
folks that will not wash. They already
know about the lawyer and the
robberies. So, I'll visit this place
and just relax.

* * *

Later, the lieutenant went over the evidence with the detective, and what the other investigators found about the case for a few minutes. It was clear that those investigators provided nothing that Wally could use. He remarked. "They found nothing that will help us find a suspect, sir."

"Yes," and then they chatted some more.

They went over the report about DNA. They found that there was a match from the two crime scenes. That matched no one in the FBI data base. That was the only evidence they had. He had nothing to go on there as well. Thus, there was nothing solid.

That and him being undercover among friends made things very clear to Detective Flore. That beings he was grasping for straws with this assignment that his lieutenant gave him. The detective was told to have a good time. His partying maybe all gets out this investigation.

The detective made a final comment to his commander just prior to the meeting ending. He remarked. "The DNA seems as like it is little to go on alone. This could turn out to be a long break for me."

"Ha just solve this thing. You detective need to cut me break. I have suffered from these damn cases long

enough."

"I'm on my way," Flore laughed.

"See you later, sir."

"Give it hell, Detective; find

those robbers, and what happened to

that lawyer, bye."

"Yes, sir, I will," and he said

goodbye, the meeting was over, and he

parted from there.

* * *

The bookie of that neighborhood,

Henry, never thought of any customer as

a criminal. That was true before he saw

him and Jimmy Collen with Cole James.

It was true even after that meeting
even it was the last time the lawyer
was seen.

Then again, he still never thought
of his bookie or his assistant, Jim
Collen, as criminals. That same bookie,
Aaron Henry, also handled the Don and
Helen Robby's income tax returns.

Then, the Aaron Henry went for a
drink at the motel bar. He was standing
at the bar pouring being poured a
second drink of Jack Daniels when he
saw Jim Collen enter the reception
room.

They each took a long hard look at
one another and did not speak as Jim

Collen approached the bar. The

bartender poured him his usual drink as

he came toward him at the end of the

bar. He pushed a bar stool away and

stood at the bar with the bookie.

They stared at one another not

going to the bother of toasting their

success. The bookie spoke first. "You

bastard, you cleaned up on basketball

season again and you're nailing

baseball! You help me and don't book

anything alone!"

"I'll give your share when we're

alone."

Now if you keep it up with these

gamblers during football season, we can

both retire well off," Jimmy left him,

and went back to working at the motel for his father.

Then Jimmy's father, a man simply known as Collen, entered the room wanting to hear that his gambling debt had been satisfied by providing the of the reception room.

He offered no bitter exchange with the bookie or his guards. Collen clearly looked like he felt cause to get violent with him. "Well that's a pretty good take when you were out for my blood."

"Hey man, you were cool about this. You could have tried to humiliate us. Your debt is off the books for the use of your reception room and providing the food too."

"Okay, don't take anymore book on my son," unaware that Jim worked at helping the bookie.

"I cut you breaks because you bring gamblers my way once they are drunk in your bar."

"I'm still pissed at you for hanging around with Jimmy."

"He's a stupid kid, but he brings me more book than you."

The bookie knew that there was no one he knew better at getting drunks aroused to bet sports than Jimmy Collen. He liked that about him. But, he did not like some things that he heard in Collen's remarks.

Collen was openly critical of the bookies for his treatment of his customer's wives and girlfriends. The bookie remarked to him about it. "So, that's all, right?"

"You'll need to just get a bunch of the men to defend this place."

"What, bar drunk to defend this place?"

"Yeah, I can prey on them."

"I want you to leave the women alone."

"Don't concern yourself whether or not I prey on their women!"

Collen did not want this man's helpers interfering with his customers especial the women. He replied. "I run

a motel guest to enjoy it the beach.
Not a place for hoodlums to interfere
with that."

He felt that Collen gave his
guards an opportunity for aggression
between them. He looked for a reason
for him to settle this thing with him
with their fist right now.

He tried to push Collen into
saying the fighting words. Then he
stopped, recalling that he had no
interest in that with him.

He was remined that he made a lot
of book at his motel bar. He felt that
it was best to let the issue go with
that in mind. "Collen, you'll see
better behavior the next time."

"Okay, my customers will have to worry about their own spouses," and he left the room.

The bookie laughed, mainly because he knew that he had scored some points with him. It amazed Collen that this hoodlum held back so coolly. Then the bookie turned to him. "Collen, I remarked about that. Some real nasty shit on you has come up at the bar too."

"You speaking to me this way is not friendly, it's gossip."

"A warning."

"Nasty gossip."

"Collen, I end up leaving his bar
with some of these women at times too,"
and laughed.

"I don't much care for your ways."

"Remember, it's only business."

"Customers and business are first
and foremost."

"I know you much better than that
pal."

"Not with you here."

"Collen, what I do to protect
what's mine is your concern too. It is
first and foremost."

"My customers are first and
foremost

"You take chances. I would take a poke at you if you were someone else. You, I know, aren't going to try to knock me on my ass."

"You're a nasty man."

"Come on at me Collen, and let's see."

"That might be just what you want. You should stay out of peoples' relationships, and the gossip."

"Okay, I really don't care most of you customers, so long as it doesn't hurt me trying to take book on your drunks."

"I suppose it's better than nothing."

"You bet yah," then they left the room shortly, and Jim Collen stayed alone.

Chapter 4

Wally Flore followed the lieutenant's orders. He got in his unmarked car and drove to the motel. It was late morning when he arrived there in the lobby of the place.

Some employees, that knew him to see, waved to him as he entered there. He was glad they were not behaving like he was there to raid the place even though his cover was already blown with him just being there.

Collen, the owner, knew that he was a cop too. It did not bother him for police to nose around there. He had police passing through there at times ever since the robbery. It was becoming routine for him to see one of them there.

Flore walked through there to the pool area. He changed into the swimsuit that the police department provided for him in the men's rest room.

He walked out toward the pool deck when he came out of there. Then he saw a newspaper box. He thought for moment. 'This will add a tourist touch to this thing.' He stopped at the box, put the money in the machine, and got a newspaper out of it.

Someone piggy backed for a free newspaper. He did not try stopping them from doing that being mindful of why he was there.

The Savannah spring, hard for some folk, did not matter to sunbathers there. The pool deck was indoors with a

clear canopy ceiling to allow for the
sun's rays.

It also housed a seafood grill,
cocktail lounge, pool table, and he saw
the juke box. He thought about that and
he purchased some iced tea at the
lounge. The bartender commented to him.
"Are you on a case, Detective?"

"How did you guess?" he laughed.

"You have your cop look about you
today."

"Perhaps I should lighten up. I'll
sing along with the music in the juke
box. That will kill me some time."

He thought about that. "Sure," and
Flore thought, 'Caught at being a cop
already.'

He walked toward the poolside
lounge chairs and saw two young men by
the bar. They were both with Jim
Collen. They came there after their
workday was over. Flore has seen them
around the neighborhood.

They seemed to work together with
Jim Collen for the bookie. That day as
they did on most days. Jim Collen
commented to them. "This wasn't too bad
of a day."

"We did all right too. We all took
better book today compared to the
usual," Jim said.

Then Jim told the bookie about it
when he joined them. He remarked.
"Jimmy, you guys assist me. I don't my
guards taking book at all."

"Yeah, well it was still good. Are you hungry enough to get something from the grill?" Jimmy asked.

"No, you're still helping your father at the motel."

"Yeah," and Jim left them to deal with his father.

"Yeah, and do you feel like a little pool?" a guard asked.

"Let's get a bite first."

"Sure," the detective heard their chatter. He wondered about what they meant by much of it.

Some of Detective Flore's neighbors have been visitors' poolside there over the years, even in the early springtime.

Several neighbors were there spending their day off by the pool, swimming, eating something from the grill, and having soft drinks or something harder. Some of them came there for breakfast or lunch and others were thinking dinner here.

Every living soul there, on the pool deck and in the roped in lounge, appeared like they knew him. There were waves and hellos from nearly all of them except Jim Collen.

Wally knew all about him. His well-off parents' finances were closing on being nearly drained, and his father cut back on funding him.

Jim Collen went to work at his father's business right after he left school. Wally remarked to him. "Hello, Jimmy, I thought your father was going to run you out of the state last year for what happened at school."

"He gave me a job instead of that."

"I see you around the Jimmy and sports bar a lot too."

"Yeah, I know people there. Excuse me, I'm playing pool right now, okay with you?"

"Really, there are only two guys here."

"I'm shooting pool with Jim and those guys," the fourth player replied to that.

"Oh, the four of you," the
detective wonders.

"Yeah, the three of us playing
pool together with Jimmy."

"Wait, you're working book in here
now, correct?"

"People don't give me money for
that."

"You take book and place bets for
people even out of state," the
detective replied.

"No, I don't," Jim replied.

"Did you take money from that
missing lawyer?"

"Yeah I did. He gave it to me.
What of it?"

"Another lie. Did you kill him over bad bets or debts?"

"Hold on, Haas!"

"You did."

"No! No!"

"Did he know that you robbed this place before you killed him?"

"No! No! Rob my father's motel? That's a bit crazy?"

"I suppose that is stretching it a bit."

"I'd say so!" Then he straightened up. "Excuse me, I'm playing pool!"

"Sure, but your pals are playing without you right now."

"I'm the fourth player."

"If there are four of you playing, why have four of these guys been shooting while you haven't taken even one shot?"

"So they are, I guess I'll play later," Jim replied, and he walked away anyhow.

"Jimmy, your lying about pool, your lying about taking book and your lying…."

"I'm lying about nothing!"

The Aaron Henry just walked in the place off the street for a late lunch, before Jim Collen stopped chatting with the detective. He asked. "Leave us alone?"

"Okay Jimmy, I'll be talking to you some more."

The Henry saw that the detective had been talking to Jimmy and he did not like him doing that. Him getting caught lying doing was more annoying to him. He commented about him. "Hello there, Jimmy. So, your Wally's friend now."

"What is it?"

"What's with you? What is that cop's problem with you?"

"He started talking with me!"

"He remarked about some shit."

"What does that mean?"

"He talked about you lying when I came in the place."

"He remarked about my old man and me."

"How can you let him do that?"

"He said it got around that my old man was going run me out of the state after I was kicked out of school," he was kidding with him.

"You should have blown him off. But you think you're too slick for that."

"He came up behind me like a tourist."

"Just work for your father or go home today."

"Ha, now I'm working for the
bastard. What can I do you out of,
pal?"

"I just told you damn it! Go the
hell home."

The detective has taken note of
this in his mind since he came in, and
he was aware that Jim Collen was an
illegal gambling suspect, a liar and
nothing more. He added that up to
nothing. There was no evidence about
him and the Cole James's mysterious
disappearance.

The detective had never been
involved in any case relating to Jim
Collen, but he found himself keeping
him under surveillance. Jim Collen
seemed to have no idea that the

detective was still watching him. It
concerned the bookie that the locals
were chatting about Jimmy even talking
to the detective.

Ellyn, Mary and Sally, a local
malpractice attorney that worked with
Cole James, arrived on the property in
street clothes. Then they were in
swimsuits on the pool deck after
changing in the ladies room.

They were scattered among the
people around the pool, mingling. Then
they normally come back together after
they are done visiting with some of
those other people.

Everyone on the pool deck was here
for different reasons. Many of them
were from around the neighborhood. Some

of them were in Savannah on business
and had no idea who this Flore might be
nor did they care about it.

The residents that were sitting
around the pool or standing around the
cocktail lounge, drinking, all wondered
what this cop was doing there. Jim
Collen's story, about what he did he or
didn't do was already around.

The Aaron Henry was chatting among
the locals and businesspeople present
alike as he was sipping champagne
before lunch with Ellyn. They finished
lunch, and sat by the pool, relaxing,
and still sipped more champagne.

Then Ellyn went over to Flore
wondering what interest the police had
with Jimmy. Mary and Sally saw her and

got up came toward them too. Ellyn

asked him about the boy. "What are you

doing Wally? Why were you bothering

Jimmy? Did he commit a crime or

something?"

"His situation doesn't add up to

me. He's making bets for people and he

has cause to commit a crime. I hoped to

catch him in a lie a little while ago.

He got away from me this time, but I'll

catch him before long."

"He wouldn't do that."

"If he tries it again, I'll be

right there to nail him," she left his

side not appreciating what he said.

She mentioned it to Mary and

Sally. Then Sally came over to Wally

Flore. She commented to him about what seems is coming down. "Detective, you're here to rattle people that are trying to have a good time. You're scaring the hell out of some of them. What are you doing here?"

"I'm waiting for my friend, Ida."

"You got on that young boy's case," Sally replied.

"Yes, I suppose I did. I just wanted to warn him about a few things."

"Watch yourself, he has rights."

"Of course," and she went back to chat with the two women that came there with her."

Then Ida arrived to visit with Wally. They got in the pool together.

Then Ellyn and Mary, got off their lawn chairs, and went in the pool. Ellyn started talking to Ida. "Is he your boyfriend or something?"

"He's a friend."

"It seems that he came here to accuse people of some crimes. You should watch that he doesn't try to arrest you."

"Are you driving?"

"No."

"It's good that you're not, you seem quite drunk. He could arrest you for that," and they laughed.

Mary has been involved in some small talk with some neighbors that were in the pool. Flore and Ida were still in the pool and he joined in on the chatting making them laugh. In a short while, he made some of the other folk's nerves. So, it was just him and Ida that were talking to one another.

Then they climbed out of the pool and sat on some lawn chairs. She enjoyed the company of this new friend and hoped that he would come on to her sexually. However, he got to look at another man that he knew as a bad boy.

Chapter 5

His sexual fraternizing with Ida that day was only for appearances, doing the job, and all the ladies knew that except her. The bookie was often jealously watching other couples. Flore saw how he was in that way toward Ida.

He felt that he could take advantage of that and perhaps catch a criminal. He kissed Ida knowing that Aaron Henry was watching. The two of them being that way just made him crazy with jealous feelings. Flore wondered about him realizing that. 'Could this bookie have been jealous of Cole James over a woman?'

Flore needed to use the restroom. He was aware that there was a men's room by the pool table. He got up from his seat with an eye on Aaron Henry. "Excuse me, nature calls."

"Sure, sweetie, hurry back," Ida said.

"I need to allow a proper amount of time for this," she laughed at that.

Flore walked toward the men's room by Aaron Henry, some of his men, along with Ellyn and Jim. Aaron Henry did nothing more than to give him a hard stare.

Then, Flore passed by another guy needing the restroom. He was a little off balance and he bumped into Aaron Henry's pool stick and he missed his shot from that. Aaron Henry rudely commented. "Hey, watch it!"

"Oh-no, you missed your shot," Flore said to Aaron Henry, and still nothing happened.

He knew that he wanted to get Aaron Henry's story about the times of the robberies. But they were no longer shooting pool when he came out of the men's room. Aaron Henry, Ellyn, Mary and Jim and went to the bar for drinks.

Flore and Ida went to the bar, and he made sure that they took seat by them. Mary commented to them. "Hello Wally and your lady."

"Hello Mary, she is Ida," Flore said.

"I've seen those guys around. They are always with him?" Flore asked Ellyn and Mary referring to Aaron Henry and some of his men.

"No, I think he just met them," Ellyn replied with a slight slur.

"You're kidding."

"You know Wally, I saw those two guys twice; both times the afternoon before those robberies around the corner," Mary said.

"Isn't that strange," Flore said.

"Yes, it sure is."

"Ellyn, you say that guy with those two guys is your boyfriend?"

"Sometimes, but he's too possessive, arrogant and jealous to get serious with him."

"So yeah and he's not getting married you?" Flore kidded her.

"Oh right," it did not seem matter to Ellyn.

"You say possessive?" Mary asked.

"Oh yeah, he is." Ellyn said. "He still thinks that he owns me, he won't be marrying me anytime soon and Wally, you got him real pissed off."

"How interesting," Flore said.

Their conversation continued with Aaron Henry and his buddies watching and talking about Flore. The detective replied to her. "He's clearly angered by someone."

"Wally, ready his lips. He just said; That damn guy is a cop. What the hell does he want here?"

"Ellyn, can guess about the other guy?" Flore asked her.

"Who knows? He's from around here?" she guessed.

"I know that much."

This bit of information told Flore that they are concerned about him. Then the waitress asked. "Are you ready to order?"

"Ida, should we eat now or later?"
Flore asked.

"I can wait to eat," and the
waitress moved on.

Aaron Henry was watching them. He
commented. "I can't hear him, and he
still makes me mad. He is making me mad
enough to take him on! Somehow I need
to kick his ass!"

"What did he do?" one of his men
asked, getting no immediate answer.

"Look at the bastard!" Aaron Henry
commented. "He's drooling over my
girl!"

"He's doing nothing."

"I would have even hated him in
school!"

"You got no need to kick ass every time someone looks at Ellyn."

"Look at her? He's with her!"

* * *

Detective Flore took out his phone. He planned to have Aaron Henry's pals discretely checked out by his station before they leave the property. He made his call about them.

Ellyn heard the call and told him what she knew about them. Flore listened to Ellyn and it was also clear that she knew something about Cole James too. "Go on Ellyn."

***ELLYN TOLD WALLY FLORE

SOMETHING THAT THE LIEUTENANT

WISHED THAT HE LEARNED EARLIER

IN THE INVESTIGATION***

"A year earlier, Jimmy Collen had been expelled from high school as a junior. Then he ran into Aaron Henry, and I was with him." He greeted him. "Hello, Aaron."

"Hi Jimmy," Aaron Henry said.

"I would have put the few dimes I have left on my old man having me run out of the state when they kicked me out of school," he was kidding with him.

"But you're too slick for that."

"Ha, yeah, right. Now, I'm working for the bastard. What do you want?"

"You know the guy that took bets at the sports bar and the diner down the street for me?"

"Really?"

"He died and I replaced him and you me."

"I still work for my father. So, why did you replace him?"

"One of the drunks told me that they need someone slick to take it over from him. He told me that some tough looking guy was who they needed."

"Listen Jimmy, you make like I didn't tell you this."

"You're slicker than me."

"The cop over there would like better than to kick my ass."

*　*　*

Aaron Henry grew up there in Savannah even though he had been born in New Orleans thirty-five years ago. He was fresh off another divorce. He was always looking for action with the young ladies. He looked a little like Clark Gable with his bushy dark hair and mustache.

Some women were more impressed with his tough and dirty arrogance rather than any gentlemanly mannerism. His power was outside the law. However, still he had always tried to appear as a man of great business secrecy acting like his legitimate endeavors give him some creditability.

Jim Collen went on lunch break from the motel job immediately. Besides, it was too nice of a day to work. He walked to the roped in area.

He took the seat next to Aaron Henry at the counter. He sat there waiting for Aaron to give his early lunch order. Jimmy Collen was still thinking about taking the afternoon off anyway and what he could do with this waitress during that time while he waited to order. The waitress took their meal order to the kitchen a moment later.

Aaron Henry turned and looked at him. "I would rather have gone to that diner down the street."

"You don't like my old man's place, Aaron?"

"I don't like being around that cop."

"Yeah, most people here are nervous about him."

"He rattles me."

Aaron thought about having Collen asking him to leave. He looked over at Flore and it rattled him more. He then thought that he better not does that. He remarked to the waitress. He said the waitress. "Fix our orders, and get them out here, and give it to him as a takeout."

Then he commented to Collen. He remarked. "Give her your order, bring me mine to my car, and give her a good tip."

"Where are you going?"

I'm taking the booking money to the bank," he gave him money to cover the cost of the whole thing.

"That has you wacked out too."

"I'll take book here in your place?"

"Not here today. Send the gamblers to other places."

"Let me get out of here?" and he got up and left there.

Henry was gone from there. Jimmy Collen began taking book in Aaron Henry's place. He was doing the opposite as Henry asked.

Jimmy Collen booked what he thought were for sure bad bets. They were in fact just that all bad picks. Flore saw the betting coming down. He was not ready to arrest anyone yet.

Then Collen left there after getting the meal orders. He said. "See you later babe."

"I'm not your babe, Jimmy!" she replied.

"I'm messing with Aaron."

"Then say it to him."

* * *

Aaron Henry had a good basketball season as a bookie around the bars of Savannah after he worked at it for half a year. He took over a small grocery store on Woodlawn Street on an IOU on a basketball bet from the grocer.

Aaron Henry sold the store's inventory to another grocer, and he got the money that was owed on the basketball bets. In turn he gave a good profit from the sales and building to the motel owner, Collen.

Then, he offered the building to Herbert Danielle, the young grocery clerk, always talked about owning a men's store, at a bargain, and he took the deal. The bargain price allowed the bank to give him a good deal on operating cash for his new men's store.

* * *

Don Robby's late parents felt proud when he chose Helen as his wife. They thought that their relationship was built on love. Early in the next year, in the afternoon, Helen and Don's wedding guest shuffled entering the warmth of the old Church.

It had been as chilly a winter as anyone could remember, but still it was a very nice day. However, it was special for Helen and Don. They got

married on that day, and it was such a

nice day for them.

* * *

Wally Flore made felt clear that

he found her as strikingly beautiful

woman with creamy-skin, slender body,

and luxuriant hair. He felt sure of

that noticing the warm glow in her

brown eyes when she smiled.   .

Ellyn went on to explain a few

things about Don and Helen a while

back. They were together and sailing on

the ocean in Aaron's boat.

Donny reached for her and then kissed her. "Hey baby, I'm glad you're here."

"Donny honey, what if Aaron found us here in his boat?"

"I'd like to make sure that he doesn't catch us sailing in his boat. I tried fine to ask him. Only that I couldn't find him to ask for it. Let's try to relax?"

"Fine, we'll try to relax."

* * *

"So, Donny and Helen took Aaron's boat on loan without asking?" Flore asked.

"There's more to it than that." Ellyn replied. "She was seeing both guys back then. Donny wasn't aware of that she was also spending time with Aaron."

"Now I wonder why they're both still alive."

"Me too."

"What happened that broke them up from three to two?"

"Donny's father held his riffle on Aaron to chase him away Don and Helen while they were out on a date."

"A bit reverse of a shotgun wedding?"

"Donny's mother found out Aaron was stealing her chance for

grandchildren. In her anger, she gave Aaron a scar in his leg with a steak knife."

"A knifing is a severe penalty for stalking. Was she arrested for doing that?"

"His parents died a short time after that from of natural causes."

"That doesn't explain why Helen isn't married to Aaron?"

"I don't know, she simply decided on Donny in the end."

"From what I can tell, I don't know the truth from gossip in some of what I heard from you."

"That's mainly because you're a cop, Wally."

"She mainly felt that way, because she was sure that Aaron Henry only just wanted sex with her. There was no love to it at all."

"You heard Helen saying that?"

"Yeah, she made it clear to me."

"Do you recall her remark?"

"Sure."

* * *

"She remarked to Aaron while at the diner. She said, "Remember your promise, please not today.""

"Okay, the hell with it!" he replied.

"There is more to this than sex, and I don't feel it from you."

"You think there is a motive to everything with you."

"What are you here for, to love me or just bed me?"

"Let's spend some time together without fighting over that."

"Sure, we could have."

"Let's spend time together. That will make you feel better."

"So, the answer is that you only want your way with me!"

"Damn it, woman I asked you to marry me months ago.""

Ellyn was openly appalled about Aaron Henry as she told Flore about him. "I saw Helen at the motel pool deck. Aaron still pursued her and me openly as well."

Then she explained more about Helen. She is a lovely and warm young lady. The spontaneity of her lovely and gentle smile glows enough to turn heads. Her skin is smooth and lightly tanned. He yelled to her. "Loveliness, you look like you're lost in this crowd."

"Helen brushed him off, but Aaron Henry laughed and did not give up, seated by her. "It's not really crowded here. You can sit somewhere else.

Besides, I'm waiting to meet with someone."

"That would be me," Aaron Henry said.

"No Aaron."

"Aaron got up and rejoined me. We were walking by her friend Sally. Sally saw right through Aaron Henry and told me so. "This guy with you is such a jerk, girl."

"You should be lucky enough to have me with you," Aaron remarked to her.

"Oh really, well I think that I'd rather be as I am."

"Sally was not fooling anyone either. She looked back at him wishing he were interest in her. She was a little annoyed and a little envious that the guy was paying all his attention on Helen and me and not her. "You are forever a jerk."

"Then a while later; I told Sally that I wanted to spend some time alone with Aaron. It appalled her, however she left us alone. He had his way with me later at my apartment. It made him so proud that he had scored on still another girl.""

"It was all about Aaron Henry, some women and jealousy?"

Ellyn continued telling the detective her story. She replied telling him more. "Helen was working a shift as a waitress at the diner. Her

customers were there having their
dinner. She had been on duty for over
an hour. Most of her customers chatted
about the latest gossip. She knew that
it was about her.

"All of them were chatting that
she agreed to marry Aaron Henry. She
was sick of hearing what she thought of
as bull about her and Aaron Henry. She
wanted to believe what he said to her
about his love for her.

"She already moved in with Aaron
Henry. She felt that she already dished
out plenty of misery on her husband now
that he was sure about her relationship
with Aaron Henry. She expected that he
would come by later that evening. She
thought that it would be her only

chance to tell him that she didn't
wanted a divorce before he heard this
gossip.

"Herb Danielle a good friend to
Helen and Aaron Henry arrived. He came
in for dinner. He could not stay long.
He had to work at his store and close
it at 9 o'clock. He gave her a hug as
he entered the diner the same as
always."

"Helen greeted him saying. "Hello
Herb," She spoke with the tone of her
voice less than cheery toward him. That
was not unusual for her. However, her
mood had more to it to him as he
greeted her."

"Hi sad eyes, something has you
down," Herb said.

"Oh, it's the talk about Aaron
Henry, Donny and me."

"Helen, I have a little time to
hear it. But, take carry of your other
customers first."

"You're a businessman like Donny
Robby. He's neurotic about this
business he got from his late daddy.
You're always calm about your shop."

"I spend hours a week sitting on a
bench viewing the ocean."

"Herb, that is sweet of you," and
she kissed him on his forehead."

Chapter 6

***ELLYN STOPPED TELLING HER

STORY THAT INCLUDED FLORE***

"Then you entered the diner,
Wally, asked her. "Where is my kiss?""

"Oh yes, I was new here as a cop."

"They had you working downtown
before then. Do you remember that
encounter?" Ellyn asked.

"Yes, Helen remarked to Herb about
me," the detective replied to her.

"Wally, do you recall what Helen
remarked to him?"

"Yes, I do, "Herb, the creeps are
coming out of the woodwork, is there a
full moon tonight?""

He laughed recalling that. She
asked. "That's all you heard?"

"Yes."

"He mentioned you, Detective."

"I didn't know."

"You were outside talking on, what I thought, was your police phone."

"I see."

"While you were outside, Herb Danielle said a few things about you, the new detective. He said that he knew you from downtown."

"Oh sure, my father knew him from here and I met him there."

"Some cop. Then you forgot him."

"He forgot me, so that is all you recall from that encounter?"

"No, he forgot your name too."

"He remembered your father."

"I told him, of course you know
me."

"Ellyn, I've been buying clothes
at Herb's Shirt Shack for a few years.
He knows me as officer or detective."

"So, your commander sent you off
somewhere and never talked to him."

"Really?"

"The gossip when you came back in
the diner. You finished eating. We said
goodbye, you left the diner and I moved
to sit at another place at the
counter."

"You're saying that Herb was
watching me. He could be aware of a lot
about these cold cases."

"Even in on some of it?"

"Ellyn, perhaps so."

"That's right, Herb. Tell more
about him."

ELLYN WENT BACK TO HER STORY

"Herb always listened to Helen
talk about her social life, however not
that day. She tried to talk about it,
but she could not bring herself to say
a word about it even to him."

"I'm sorry Herb, I would talk to
you about this, but I can't. Except
that it's my business and not of these
customers or people on the street that

are gossiping about it," that was all
that Helen said about it.

"Oh, your customers here are
talking about you and Aaron Henry too?"

"Yes, but it is between us."

"Sure, and Donny. I'm going to get
out of here. Goodbye Helen, and he
stood up to leave there."

"I was already gone?"

"Yes, Detective Flore. He watches
you and asked about you when you're at
the diner."

"Is he with Aaron Henry or Jimmy
Collen very much?"

"Yes, Detective. You were there when the three of them sat in booths together."

"Really, and I didn't nab the bad guys."

"No, you allow me to finish."

"Please do, I have all day."

"I don't like talking about Aaron, Helen and Donny at all. Hell, Aaron was my guy before Helen."

"This chat really hurts you."

"No, it annoys me."

"Lets just chat a little more."

Ellyn explained to him more about the gossip Helen and Aaron Henry before she broke up with Aaron Henry. She

replied. "Herb came in the diner
talking gossip with several people.
That told Helen that it wasn't just
Aaron Henry. The talk about her getting
married to him. It got around on the
street too."

"It was Donny?"

"I heard nothing about him in that
way. She never thought he did that. She
did think that they were chatting about
them in line at Webb's Bakery too. She
did not want to hear anyone's two cents
about it not even from Aaron Henry."

"You mean that Aaron Henry first
learned about that on the street? He
didn't hear it online. He listened to
her deny it all right?"

"She knew that Aaron Henry had several girl friends that he treated like whores, like me."

"I can't arrest him because you're mad that Helen took him from you."

"Helen explained how she felt about it to me. She only brings these people their meals. I surely do not want to spend my time listening that gossip there."

"She doesn't like the gossip and doesn't who he marries?"

"Donny's pretty much the biggest chump around. He was not one to interfere in any ones affairs of the heart even to try saving his marriage. He felt that Helen could work things

out for herself. He also owes Aaron
Henry a gambling debt. He and Herb both
owe him on sports betting."

"Helen did not see Donny enter the
diner, but I did. Then they were face
to face after she turned around after
taking an order. I could see that she
had the look of sorrow all over her
face. I could tell that he expected
that she wanted a divorce. She still
could not say the words about it. Then
he stood in front of her and asked.
"You want a divorce, don't you?"

"So, they're getting divorced?"

"She did not say yes to him,
Wally. She just kind of nodded her head
yes. He looked drained of everything
that moment. He looked through his

wallet and found a business card that he got from his late father years ago. Then he spoke again. "We each need a lawyer to handle this." She finally spoke, saying "We'll see."

"I saw him hand her the card, and I heard the rest. This will be my lawyer," he said.

"Aaron, we were never really soul mates," Helen said.

"That's it in a nutshell, we're not soul mates. So that justifies you constantly cheating on me with Aaron Henry."

"Whatever it was Aaron, I'm glad that you don't want me anymore."

"Baby, I know that you can't learn to love me. I can't believe that you believe that Aaron Henry will ever love you. The bastard only loves himself and that is it."

"Fine Donny, I have an appointment with a lawyer, and I'll give her this card."

"Sure."

"One thing more, I'm so sorry, Donny," and they both walked out of the diner, her through the front door, him the back after locking up.""

Ellyn had more to tell the detective. However, she wanted to know why he knew so little about what happened. "Wally, you were on those streets back then?"

"Yes, I was there."

"Well why do I have to tell everything that happened then? What were you doing? It seems you were ignoring the streets or something."

"Wow, that's shot across the bow. I was doing just that. Otherwise, we wouldn't have turned all of these cases as cold as they are."

* * *

Wally had his own story about Ellyn. He began telling it to her. He said. "Ellyn, I have all day, of course, to tell you this. About six months ago, Aaron Henry entered the sports bar."

"I suppose that I was there too?"

"He and the owner had a short chat in passing one another. You stepped in on them, breaking it up."

"They parted, with Aaron Henry walking toward a bar stool." Ellyn Replied to the detective. "He commented to me. He remarked. "Hello Ellyn. Did you pick his pocket when you ran into him?"

"Ha." Ellyn replied to Aaron. "That's a good one. You and I should talk."

"Sure, let's have a drink together.""

"I suppose it seemed like a good plan to each of you." Wally pointed out to her. "So, you pointed at seats in the corner. Those seats are pretty private, about same place as where Aaron and I sit."

"Yes, you notice that Jimmy Collen was seated looking over the book he took, during the day, in the booth across from there."

"Yeah, what of it?"

"Aaron and you were about to sit in those seats!"

"Okay, he and I still hookup!"

"Collen came to him to chat for a moment."

"Jimmy or the old man?"

"Collen is always the old man."

"It was the father."

They laughed about the name thing. You remarked to Aaron Henry. She remarked. "Wally, I suppose you want to sit elsewhere?"

"We can stay here until I feel that I learned enough."

"Let's sit elsewhere."

"He'll stay put if we do."

"Why do you say that?"

"He's too rattled to move with a cop here. You stay seated with him will annoy him more and rattle him less."

"If you're so smart where do you think he's going with this?"

"You ask him?"

"Well, I suspect that he's not marrying Helen or you in the end."

"He surely doesn't love either one of us?"

ELLYN THOUGHT THAT SHE WAS FINISHED TELLING HIM HER STORY ABOUT THE DAY THAT COLE JAMES DISAPPEARED

Chapter 7

Detective Flore took his phone out a moment later. He planned to have Aaron's pals discretely checked out by officers before they leave the property. Then Ellyn made a strange comment about one of them. "That guy, I saw him kill him."

That amazed Mary hearing it. She remarked. "Come on Ellyn, you don't mean that."

"I really do."

"You couldn't have seen it."

Flore listened to Ellyn and it was also clear that she knew something about what happened to Cole James. He asked. "What happened, Ellyn?"

"I was across the street from him when he shot his tire, and he crashed into the ocean!" she was getting angry recalling it.

"Which one did it?" Flore asked Ellyn.

"Wally that guy robbed those motels!" Mary replied.

"You are a son of a bitch!" Ellyn yelled at one of the local men.

The people on the partly crowded pool deck looked toward these women sitting with Flore. They wander about what was exciting them. Flore was confused by her too. He asked. "Who is it?"

"Him!" Ellyn pointed at the crowd.

"Really?"

"Yes!" Mary said.

Flore called his station for backup as he watched, listened, and questioned them. Then he asked. "There are a number of men in the crowd. Be specific?"

"You killed him, didn't you, you bastard!" Ellyn yelled.

"Who is he?" Flore asked again.

Ellyn kept yelling at some guy that she suspected. But she did not point him out to Flore. "Are you going to murder more people?"

Flore thought that the guy was confessing when he heard his first few words of response. "I did it." But, he had more to say as he stumbled to try to speak with authority. "You mean…what-t? You think I committed some crimes?"

"You're the damn bastard that killed our dear friend after you robbed all those places," Ellyn's words of anger kept coming out her mouth directed at him.

Flore could not believe that several unsolved crimes were being solved as these women let it be known that they witnessed them. He stared right at Jimmy Collen as he walked toward the men's room thinking it was, he. "Ellyn, point him out! Oh wow, he is here!"

"It's him!" Mary yelled and pointed at Jimmy.

Ellyn and Mary point at different guys that were walking toward the restroom at the same time. "No, Jim!" Ellyn yelled.

"No, it's not him!" Mary yelled.

Detective Flore was still dumfounded about it and yelled out. "What?" He yelled. "Wow! It's Aaron Henry isn't it?"

The detective has made a few surprise discoveries while checking crime scenes prior to this. He has not been involved in these investigation type cases until now.

He has only been part of the team trying to get the goods in these cases. But he was now overjoyed, and shock that he was taking him down.

Ellyn was devastated as she looked face to face at this guy. Aaron Henry saw that and walked for the door to exit the motel.

He knew that Ellyn was drunk and hysterically as she explained that he was the real killer. "That murderous scum is his killer! I watched him do it and I did nothing!"

Flore knew that no weapon was found. "Aaron Henry, hand me your gun now!"

"Yeah, I saw him!" Ellyn broke down crying, and hugged Flore.

When Flore was finished hearing that, he was nothing short of being amazed with getting such eyewitness confessions. The police have seemly lucked out to have witness proof that identified the robber and Cole James's killer.

They still had no physical evidence other than the DNA on that iPod that was found the other day. Flore hoped to get a match there. He would see to it that it would be

checked against the DNA of these
suspects.

Flore heard the sirens of his
backup police officer's cars arriving
moments later. They shut their sirens
and got out of their cars with flashing
lights on the roofs.

They rushed toward the pool deck
and saw Flore. He directed them toward
Aaron, Jimmy, and others. "That's them.
Take all four of them to jail in
handcuffs."

"What is this?" Jimmy's father
asked annoyed.

"That's him! He robbed the motels
and the guy with him too!" Mary said.

"No, you can't take my boy!"
Jimmy's father said.

Then Flore held Ellyn for a while
longer and asked her some questions
about what happened on the night that
Cole James was killed as the police
officers put the suspects in handcuffs.
"How do you know this about Jimmy
killing?" his father asked.

"I remember seeing him following
Cole that night."

"O, he followed Cole James. Still
there is no body, and no weapon. What
ties him to a murder?"

"He is the same man I saw run out
of the bar right after Cole got in his
car."

"Yes good, what else happened?"

Aaron Henry had connection with the mob. However, he was not a part of it. These arrests have put him out in the open exposing him and them to the law enforcement.

It is dangerous for Aaron Henry with relationship with them. Flore was as amazed that the three young men that worked for him were suspects in different crimes. He thought. 'What the hell happened?'

Then Aaron Henry saw Flore point him out to officers. He looked at each officer in disbelief. He saw that he was trapped there. Then they put handcuffs on him.

He arrogantly pushed away from them, and walked over to Ellyn, and remarked. "Ellyn, you know that we're not the motel, and convenience store robbers. Are you giving us up trying to pick up this detective?"

Ellyn did not answer him. She commented to the ladies, and Detective Wally Flore. "You see what I mean about that jerk."

The detective felt lucky to catch Aaron Henry, and his men particularly with them not even considered suspects. He still had another surprise for them. Flore commented to Aaron Henry about it. "Aaron Henry, I have no idea if you committed these crimes until we check your DNA. It never occurred to me to check you out with the computer for prior warrants for your arrests."

"You'll find nothing. This whole thing is about you and the girl."

"You other boys, do you think there are prior warrants on you?"

Flore laughed when they did not reply to him. Then he commented to an officer. "Officer, check these four suspects in the computer for priors before you take them away."

"Yes sir," the officer said

"Good," and Jimmy's father pleaded with him to let son go free.

Aaron and his men knew what was happening, and it worried him. Flore stepped in front of Aaron Henry. He commented. "Have a seat for a few minutes Aaron. It won't be too long until we have our computer check completed."

Aaron sat down doing nothing more. He the expecting to join the other three leaving there for the trip to the county jail in handcuffs.

The first uniformed officer finished getting priors on the young men from the police computer. Flore noticed that he had the reports of what he found. He asked. "Officer, what do you have on these fine young men?"

"Detective Flore, they are all wanted on prior warrants for other crimes."

"Well Aaron, do you think that your drunkard girl's evidence will get tossed by the DA?" Flore asked with no answer. "You boys are all wanted in Indiana. How's the song go? Indiana wants me," and he sang a bit of that song.

The officer also found that three of them were all wanted on outstanding warrants for violation of their probation in Florida. "When we're done with you, the three of you are going to Orlando, Florida for three hot meals (prison meals), and a cot there."

"Jimmy, you don't get to go to Florida with your friends. You won't get to spend a day at the beach. Well, Orlando is not the beach. Actually,

none of you will ever see the beach
again."

Soon, a police van arrived there
to take the suspects to jail. The
officers began to walk them toward the
exit door.

Flore said nothing more to them.
He just pointed at the door to for the
uniformed officers to take them all to
the county jail, and they walked to the
waiting van; outside. Then the police
put them in the van. A few minutes
later, the van drove off with four of
them going to jail.

Those guests, from Savannah crowd,
on the pool deck, were accustomed to
strange arrests in the tougher
neighborhoods. But they lived where

crime was particularly low a year ago. The five robberies and missing lawyer changed that.

Wally Flore did not see the significance of his arrest for those crimes. His real hope against the suspects was not the Savannah crimes or that of the prior warrants. He hoped that the Florida probation violations would keep them locked up for a couple years each.

He knew that Ellyn's only real help was that he got to check out a connected hood, and some of his friends with the computer. He asked her about what she told him. "Ellyn, how does this story help our case?"

"I saw Cole James at the diner."

"He was also at the bar across from there, and at his law office before that. Tell me about all of this?"

Ellyn was devastated as she looked at Flore. He saw that. He expected no more answers at that meeting with her. He walked toward the door to exit as the van was being loaded. Ellyn got hysterically yelled at these suspects. "That murderous scum killed him!"

"We'll have him in jail soon."

"I know that he fired that gun and I did nothing to stop him!"

"Jimmy Collen has a gun?"

"Yeah, I know he does!"

"He was unarmed when we arrested him."

She broke down crying, and hugged Flore. When he was finished hearing her, he felt that these women had their own ulterior motives about the four suspects and may have given false eyewitness confessions. "How do you know this about Aaron Henry, and the other men?"

"I remember seeing them on the TV news some time ago."

"But, how does that tie them to these crimes?"

"He was talking to the same man I saw run out of the sports bar after that woman who got beaten."

"Yes, but these crimes occurred
before that," he was unsure of what
these witness said, and they were
drunk.

Chapter 8

The next day, he brought the
witnesses to his office to hear it
again. Ellyn and Mary told the
detective what they really knew about
the cases.

Ellyn did not even recall that she spoke of a tire shooting and a gun a day earlier. The witnesses said that they enjoyed Cole James's celebration at sports bar six months earlier.

The two girls chatted, laughed, and hugged as they reminisced about the party as they got ready to go home. Then Cole James drove them home from there.

He was very drunk when he climbed into the driver's seat. They pull out of the street parking space, drove up the street, and he made a right turn, and then left one after they went one block.

Ellyn thought she noticed that he missed a turn lost in his own neighborhood. She said. "You made a right when you should have made a left."

"A left really?" Cole replied. "We're going home incorrectly?"

He was a bit disoriented hearing conflicting instructions from them with them being so drunk too. He was not sure of where they were going anyway. However, he thought he was sure. "What? Sure, I'm going the right way."

They rode up their street and stopped in front of their apartment building. He held the door for them dropping them off there, and they each kissed him good night.

He got back on the road to head
for his apartment on the Atlantic Ocean
front. That was all that they knew
about him.

The police detectives finally
found that they had no case against any
of the suspects that Flore arrested.
Only Jimmy Collen was released from
jail. The others remained in jail with
the prior warrants being processed, and
then the Florida charges.

* * *

The lieutenant called Detective
Flore to his office to inform him of
the captain's decision. The detective

stood in his doorway a short time later. "Hello, sir."

"I have problems with all our cases," the detective made some remarks as he entered the office, and they chat some more.

The lieutenant tried to discuss the problem at hand. He said. "You need to help me with this."

"Of course, I will, sir."

Flore was serious, but the lieutenant did not see any chance of them breaking the backs of these cases. The lieutenant explained a few things to him. "The charges are not sticking, and I need to keep these suspects in jail."

"I have helped you with that, sir. Florida and Indiana want Aaron Henry and two of his men. We are sending them to Florida, and they won't be going fishing out on the ocean again."

"That sounds good."

"Those two drunkard women are crazy, but their lies gave us the opening to check Aaron Henry and company for the prior outstanding warrants. We hit the jackpot with Florida. Their probation violation involves to escapes from police stations. They will do four years for that. Then they get charged in Indiana."

"Great work Detective. Still we have those six neighborhood crimes, and their DNA doesn't match that on the iPod."

"Yes, I'm working on it sir."

"I suppose you are doing that. Well I need you full time on the case until we break the back of these robbers."

"I can do that for a while."

"Okay, I think that we understand one another."

Flore could tell that the lieutenant was obviously holding back his frustration with the detective's leisure time undercover assignment not producing the robber or what really happen to the missing lawyer.

Three of the detective's suspects will serve several years in jail out of state for at least the probation violates in Florida. That is face saving for the detectives cases even if he charged them for none of his case crimes.

The lieutenant knew that his problem was that he should have used this detective on the investigation from the beginning.

He also knew that sending him on the cases so late was proving, at best, as saving face to his superiors. He explained his problem with them to Flore. "Detective, I need to depend on you."

"What assignment do you want me to handle?"

"Wally, I need you on the motel and convenience stores robberies and stay undercover to find out what happened to that lawyer. We lost our window with so much leg dragging. Then I hoped that you would flush out those hoods for our cases. We can't say that the cases are solved."

Flore was also aware that these cases have been going nowhere, and the lieutenant was feeling the heat from his superiors again even with Aaron Henry off the streets. "Sir, I know that you don't need to feel any more pressure."

"Wally, I suppose I hit a nerve with you. It's not your failure at all. With all this crime in Savannah, I think you did well for the neighborhood by bringing down the Aaron Henry's hoodlums. But listen Detective, keep spend your time visiting these undercover spots on this list. There are places to check on. Do it until you get a lead, and then I know that you'll eat up these cases."

This was clearly Flore's most affective kind of assignment to him, where he mixed his feel for the neighborhood with the detective business. "Who said that you don't love me, sir?"

"You know I just want these cases solved."

"Like you said, we missed our window."

"Try your best."

The lieutenant told the detective what the other investigators all thought about the case for a few minutes, and then they chatted some more.

The lieutenant made a final comment as the meeting ended. He said to him. "Give it hell, Detective; find those robbers, and what happened to the lawyer, bye."

It was already clear to Detective Flore that he was grasping at straws with this assignment that the lieutenant gave him. All he could do was piece something together when he had nothing solid to go on. There was really no reason to do surveillance at most of the places on the list that he was given.

The lieutenant was convinced that the investigation needed to expand to check out more possible scenarios. He has had enough of his people investigating just a few places.

He now wanted them to check out people other than just those he knew best. They were all the obvious possibilities, and this investigation needed more teeth than that.

Chapter 9

Don and Helen Robby managed to remain married, pay the diner employees without fail and most of their personal bills. They got back some cash register stolen money taken by Jim Collen.

Don entered the diner front door.
He looked the inside of the place over
once again. Detective Flore informed
him that the bookie is on his way out
of state to jail elsewhere. He remarked
to him. "Aaron Henry's bookie joints
are closed. He's on his way to jails
elsewhere. You have no more debts with
him or any of his hoodlums that we just
arrested, the diner is yours."

"Helen told me that."

"Ellyn told me that Helen's back
with you?"

"Yeah, our marriage is on again."

"Great."

"Wally, are you on stakeout here?"

"My commanders have on stakeout everywhere."

"It looks like a perpetual vacation," Helen remarked coming out of the kitchen.

"I have to go in the kitchen," Don replied.

He glad for his cooks. He knew that his help would not have to find a job working somewhere else. He dreaded the thought of losing them.

He saw one of his cooks, one with many years there, still at work. He heard that there would be an entirely new crew Aaron Henry took it over.

He could barely look the cook in the eyes as he thought about his involvement with the cooks losing their jobs. He thought about how sorry of a man he was. Then he commented to him about his feeling. "I wish that I could do better by you. I've been pretty stupid."

"It's a tough business."

"It's even tougher when you work for someone like me who supports a bookie. I'm so sorry."

The cook told him what he already knew about what happened a few streets from there. He explained that Aaron Henry had been arrested for those robberies. "I betted on games with Aaron Henry too. Wally told me that Aaron and two of his hoods are wanted in Florida."

"Yeah, I'll bet Helen won't bail out him from there."

"No bail and those robberies are still cold cases."

"You still got her back."

"Yeah, Aaron making book is all over."

Chapter 8

The detective had been trying to make some sense of why Cole James disappeared and those cold robberies. He has not visited Ida since they were visiting that motel.

Less than a week later, Detective Flore visited Ida. He found her packing her things to leave there to return to Atlanta to visit some relatives at her former home. The detective had been away from her that long. He asked her about her packing. "Hi Ida. Are you going somewhere?"

She told him that it was a whirl wind romance. She replied. "Our whirl wind romance seems to have ended while you were investigating Aaron Henry."

"I thought we had a better chance at truly being lovers when we first met."

"There is something about you being a cop."

"Really?"

"I'm not sure why."

"I heard that damn it!"

"Wally, I'll think about you and me while I'm in Atlanta."

"If you think that, then just leave here for now?"

"That's kind of my plan."

"I hope it's only one last fling in Atlanta."

"It wasn't in my thoughts."

"Well, I should warn Ida about last flings. Don't forget Helen and Aaron."

"A fling with a hoodlum is a horrible mistake."

"Yes, nearly married that connected guy."

"Yes, I'm aware of that."

"Aaron was wanted in Florida and Indiana when we arrested him. The mob doesn't care how dirty their hoodlums are. They don't want you getting caught. If Aaron Henry was part of the mob, they would have killed him by now."

"I didn't know that he was dirty like that."

"You knew about it. Aaron had Jimmy Collen helping him take book for

him this past year. He had guards that
were really hoodlums too."

"I suppose I did know about all of
them in the end."

Ida recalled that Jimmy Collen
claimed that he came into some money
about the time of the robberies. She
remarked. "I remembered him saying that
while talking to one of Aaron's
hoodlums. So, do you think he did all
of that? Wally, does that make me a
witness?"

"What do you know about it?"

"The police were up the street
checking everything out. I never knew
that he lost at betting on sports. So,
you think he robbed those stores and

his father's motel to pay off his gambling debt?"

"Of course, he might have."

The scenario hit Flore between the eyes. He called the lieutenant about it. A DNA check was performed on him, and it matched the iPod.

* * *

Six months earlier, Cole James was thought abducted and then murdered up the street. The police believed that robberies at a motel, and the stores were committed by that murder. They were convinced that the murder victim was killed because he could identify the robber.

That case had been bogged down
without a clue. Flore was searching for
evidence that could tie the case
together. The investigation police
lieutenant, again, felt a good amount
of pressure from the captain.

Earlier in the day, a Savannah
tugboat was getting ready to haul a
barge full of cargo north on the
Atlantic Ocean coast toward the inlet
for the Savannah River. Captain Josh
the routinely carried cargo on his
tugboat. "We're picking up a barge with
a large amount of cargo. We're taking
it north of here."

The tugboat began pulling the
barge full of cargo late in the
afternoon. It was moving north offshore

only far enough out that it was still
visible in the horizon. The tugboat
captain expected to pass the inlet to
the Savannah River within the hour.

The tugboat crew was rattled by
the barge not moving at all. A seaman
yelled to captain. "Josh, what
happened?"

"Damn! Hang on crew!" Captain Josh
yelled back.

"We're being pulled ashore!" a
seaman yelled.

"The barge got snagged on
something."

Captain Josh's tugboat was
overpowered as it stopped pulling the
barge forward. The tugboat engine was

gunned however it was completely stopped by the barge. He yelled at the crew. "Stop the engines!" they stopped with the tugboat drifting into the barge.

"Skipper, we hit the barge, and it stopped us!" a seaman yelled.

"Damn!" Captain Josh yelled back to him.

"The barge is still stuck, sir!"

"Let's jump on the barge and inspect it!" Captain Jose yelled. The captain and a seaman jumped on it. He saw that the barge was stuck on a car windshield, and the car stuck on large rocks.

They saw that there had been a car wreck that ended with it on those rocks in Atlantic Ocean. All hopes of any rescues were clearly long lost. They call emergency anyway. A rescue crew came to the scene before the police arrived.

They reported that there were no survivors with only a small amount of investigation. A diver crew reached the car underwater. They retrieved a single victim. The dead man's body that they removed was Cole James.

* * *

Six months earlier, James was trying to drive home. He drove around the block and around block again and again until he thought he saw his apartment building.

He did not reach his home on Atlantic Ocean. Then he looked ahead noticing something. He did not realize that he somehow ended up on the wrong side of the Savannah River.

He kept driving anyway. He kept doing it even though he felt he was lost. He thought he must have a wrong turn if was on the wrong side of the river.

Where the hell am I, he wondered? Mary insisted that I made the correct

turn at the end of their street. No,
that was when I took them home.

I guess I turned left when it
should have been right. He was annoyed
with his error. Oh damn, how the hell
did I get here?

He did not realize that a sign
said not to cross the road. He drove
the car across the road with no regard
for that. His car ran over the sign,
and he drove on, not across the bridge,
over a steel merchant ship dock.

The car crashed into Atlantic
Ocean at the inlet for the Savannah
River. It plunged to the bottom of the
ocean shipping lane quickly. However,
the victim could not figure out how to

open the car door to get out of it just after the car hit the ocean.

So, he went down with it. The drunken lawyer could not save himself from drowning. No one saw the car crash into the ocean. So, nothing was done to attempt to rescue him during the entire process.

* * *

The captain of the neighborhood police department was walking into the station a few minutes later and recognized the commissioner immediately.

There was concerned in his face that he was making a surprise inspection of his police station. The captain snapped at the officer at the desk. "What is he doing here?"

"He is being held for possible charges of involuntary manslaughter," the officer said.

"Give me what you have on this manslaughter," the captain was clearly shocked to hear that.

He reviewed the statement that orders an arrested for the manslaughter charges, "This isn't the commissioner."

"No sir. That's the manslaughter suspect," he pointed at a man in hand cuffs. "I want to know about why the commissioner is here?"

"The missing lawyer's body was
found in his car in Atlantic Ocean,"
the officer said.

"Really?"

"Yes sir."

The End.

www.ingramcontent.com/pod-product-compliance
Lightning Source LLC
Chambersburg PA
CBHW020340160726
47992CB00004B/1894